Symbolic Death

Helen Vivienne Fletcher

Copyright

First published in this format by HVF Publishing in 2020

Copyright © Helen Vivienne Fletcher, 2017

Copyright

Original and modified cover art by NaCDS and CoverDesignStudio.com

Edited by Jess Senior

"Mondegreen" was first published in Landfall 231.

ISBN:
978-0-473-50824-1 (paperback)
978-0-473-50820-3 (large print)

Dedication

For my mum, who was there when most of these stories were born.

Short-Lived Happiness

I found a butterfly chrysalis hanging from the tree outside my back door while I was feeding Alex. It was green with gold flecks, like a bejewelled bean pod.

Alex sat at my feet and watched it swishing back and forth in the breeze. He tilted his head to the side and his mouth curved up, taking him from Burmese to Cheshire.

Later, he climbed on my lap and slid the end of his tail across my throat as I sat at the computer researching butterflies. His claws dug into my thighs and I gave up looking before I figured out whether to expect a monarch or a red admiral.

I checked the chrysalis every morning after that. And every morning Alex wound his way around my legs, reminding me my job is to feed him not to stare at the trees.

One morning Alex was nowhere to be seen, but he'd left me a present – stolen chop bones on the door mat. At least it was better than the day before when he left me a dead mouse.

I picked the bones up with the very tips of my fingers and dropped them in the bin. "Thanks Alex," I muttered.

I looked for the chrysalis. It was gone. In its place hung a twist of orange and black, like a wilted nasturtium.

I held my breath.

The wings stretched, inching out from their wrinkled state. They grew, shuddering as they began to beat. My eyes felt wet and I smiled. In a flicker it took flight.

Alex jumped from behind the bushes.

"Alex, no!"

His jaws clamped.

"Alex!"

He trotted over to me and laid the mashed wings at my feet. Another present. He smiled up at me, expecting praise.

I sighed. "Thanks Alex."

Underneath the Clock

Angus kept to the centre of the corridor, tightrope-walking his feet along the gap in the lino where all the fluff got stuck. Normally, it was too busy for him to do that but, since he was leaving class early, the corridors were empty.

Angus had only been called to the office once before, but that was last year, and so he hadn't been allowed to walk there by himself. Miss Periwinkle, from reception, had come and got him. She had talked to him as they walked, and so Angus had been distracted and hadn't known he was going to find out a BAD THING. It was only when he got to the office, and he saw his mum and his brother waiting, that he knew they were going to tell him something sad.

Now Angus was in Year Two, not Year One, and Year Twos were allowed to walk to the office by themselves. Sometimes. Mostly only if the teacher was busy and they weren't in trouble.

Last year, Angus had sort of known his dad was sick. He had only sort of known, though, not really known and so the BAD THING was a BIG SHOCK. That's why Angus never cried about it. At least that's what all his teachers told him.

It's okay to cry, Angus, they said.

Then: *You've had a BIG SHOCK, haven't you?* when he didn't do any crying.

The teachers really seemed to think he should cry. They didn't understand that Angus didn't have any tears inside him. They always looked at him with their heads tilted to the side when they said BIG SHOCK, and so Angus did the same. Now whenever he thought about his dad, he thought about his neck hurting.

Angus' brother Bede was waiting outside the office. Bede's shirt was untucked, and he didn't have his tie done all the way up. He wasn't wearing his spiky cuff, though, because this morning their mum had said: *Take that stupid thing off, Bede!* and Bede had put it back in his room, muttering to himself in a quiet voice that wasn't really that quiet.

Bede had said lots of bad words when their mum couldn't hear him. Angus had heard the words though, and they made his tummy do flip-flops.

Bede looked up when Angus sat down next to him. "You in trouble too, Gussy?"

Angus shook his head.

Bede grinned. "Must just be me then, eh?"

Angus didn't think Bede should be grinning if he was in trouble, but then maybe it was just one of those pretend in-troubles. Like when their mum yelled at them for not doing things she hadn't told them to do. Then they had to say pretend-sorries, and pretend mean-it.

"Bede!" Their mother rushed into the office. She was wearing a hat, but little fluffy curls stuck out around her neck. She wasn't wearing any make up, either. "Is it true? Were you smoking?"

Angus looked at his brother. Bede swallowed and opened his mouth to speak, but their mother's face crumpled.

"The ONE thing, Bede. The ONE THING I asked you never to do." Her eyes went wide then narrowed as they teared up.

Angus tried to close his ears against his mother yelling, but she was being TOO LOUD. Her words hit him like bits of hail.

"What would I do if you got sick, Bede? What would I do? And what if you get expelled? Oh God, you're going to be expelled. Don't talk to me, Bede, I am too angry. How COULD you? I swear I have NEVER been this angry."

"Mrs Payton?" The principal, Mr Dumpty appeared in the doorway. His eyes flicked between the three of them, like a lizard pretending it was a rock. "I hope I'm not interrupting anything?"

"No ... of course not." Their mother smiled. She stood up straight, turning herself into a make-believe ballerina. She made the angry lines in her face go away, and she fluffed at her skirt with her hands.

Angus felt like he couldn't see her messy hair anymore. He knew it was there but she was acting tidy and so she almost looked it.

Angus stared at the floor beneath his feet. She was back to being outside-mum now. The one who was always perfect and never yelled.

***

When they got home, Angus took his guinea pig Bruno outside. Bede and their mum had been making angry-faces all the way home in the car, which meant it was time for Angus to go play outside.

He carried Bruno up the bank next to the garage. The bank stretched all the way up to the very top, and Angus could easily climb over the low wall and on to the garage roof. He wasn't allowed to do that though. Instead he sat down, straddling the wall, and dangled his feet over the edges. The metal roof was hot-hot-hot, burning his bare foot. His other toes were cold, where they squished the grass and mud on the bank.

He heard his neighbour, Cassie, climbing up. Cassie dangled her feet down too, but Angus could see hers didn't reach the roof.

"Let me hold Bruno." She reached out to take the guinea pig from him.

"No." Angus gathered Bruno up in his lap.

Cassie frowned and crossed her arms. "You never let me hold him." Her lips fell into a pout. She had a blotch of chocolate on her face which she rubbed at, smearing it all over her cheek.

"You're too little." Angus glanced up at the house. There'd been a CRASH from inside. "You should go home," he said to Cassie.

Cassie kicked her foot against the wall and screwed up her face. She took one of the mushy camellia flowers from the bank and pulled it apart. The petals went all pulpy and dribbled gooey-stuff down her arm.

Angus gathered a handful of grass and fed it to Bruno. He watched Cassie watching him.

She dropped the flower onto the wall. "I saw your brother," she said and stuck her thumb in her mouth.

She stretched out her other hand and let Bruno lick it.

Angus didn't look up. He pressed his little finger against one of the stones stuck in the top of the wall. It was smooth and hot from the sun, shaped like a tiny grey teaspoon. He ran his palm over it, making his hand go hot too.

"He was smoking." Cassie's voice was wet around her thumb. Her cheeks were pinky-sunburn-red. Angus rubbed the back of his neck and the skin peeled off into little grey rolly-bits.

Cassie chewed on the end of one of her plaits. "He's not supposed to smoke." She nodded to herself.

"Don't tell your mum," Angus said.

Cassie's eyes went wide. "Why not?"

Angus didn't answer. He shook his head back and forth, making a big NO.

Cassie stared at him. She took her thumb out of her mouth and wiped it on her dress. "Can I hold Bruno?"

Angus frowned at her. He picked up the guinea pig and placed him on her lap. "Don't let him climb down."

Angus stared up towards the house, but the curtains were closed.

"Why are you outside?" Cassie pulled on Angus' sleeve. "Angus?" she said when he didn't answer.

Angus shrugged.

"You never play outside anymore. You're always inside."

Angus made his face make a smile. His lips felt tight, like play dough that had got old and crusty.

The front door swung open, bashing against the outside wall. Bede stormed out of the house and down the path.

"Bede, come back here!" Angus' mother came outside. She had no shoes on and her hair stretched out around her like it was trying to run away. "Bede!" She picked her way down the path, her toes curling up away from the concrete.

Bede turned and threw a cigarette packet at her. The sun made the spiky cuff around his wrist go flash-flash-flash. "Just take them!" The cigarettes spilled out on the ground.

Angus watched as their mother covered her face. He heard her start to cry.

"Mum?" Angus said.

His mother looked up, dropping her hands from her face. "Angus," she said. Her voice had puffs of air around it, making it into a whisper. She knelt down and gathered up the cigarettes. "It's getting late," she said. "You should take Cassie home now."

Angus looked at Cassie. She was crying too.

"I dropped Bruno," she said.

***

Bede didn't come back until late. Their mum sat at the table, saying bad words under her breath. When the big hand got to 12 and the little hand got to 9, Bede still wasn't home and Mum was still sitting at the table.

Angus wasn't allowed to use the microwave, because last year he had made popcorn and used a twisty tie to close the bag and there had been a fire. Angus had been in BIG TROUBLE, but Bede was in EVEN BIGGER TROUBLE because he had been supposed to be in charge.

Mum said: "Not hungry," when Angus put the plate of toast and cold baked beans in front of her. He left it there anyway, until the bread soaked up the sauce and went red-mushy.

It was big hand on the 6 and little hand on the 10, when Bede finally came home. He patted Angus on the head. "You okay, Gussy?"

Angus swallowed. His throat was dry and scratchy. "Mum's–"

Bede shook his head. "She's okay, little man. Just go to bed." Bede looked through the glass door to the dining room, but he didn't go in. Instead he went into his bedroom and closed the door.

***

In the middle of the night, the crucifix on the wall outside Bede's room made big dark shadows on the wall. Angus thought he could see them moving, swooping down to eat his bare feet. He shuffled backwards, letting the ends of his pyjama pants cover his toes.

Angus shivered, even though he felt all hot-and-sweaty. He lifted up his hand to knock on Bede's door, but then he stopped and let his arm fall all the way back down.

"Bede?" he said. His voice came out very quiet. "Bede?" he said again, but it didn't come out any louder. He turned the door knob.

Bede's curtains were drawn, leaving only a little-tiny-bit of light creeping in through the gap. Angus squinted. He could just see Bede; a lump of arms-and-legs-and-blanket on the bed.

Angus shifted. Bede's foot was a pale blob, poking out from under the covers. Angus thought about yanking it. He turned the light on, instead.

Bede squirmed and groaned, covering his eyes. "Angus, what the hell?"

"You have to..." Angus' tongue felt thick. His words disappeared in the sticky bits of saliva in his mouth.

Bede buried his head in his pillow. "Piss off."

Angus stared at the foot sticking out from under the covers. "Bede–"

"What do you want?" Bede put his arm over his eyes, squinting out at Angus.

Angus stared at the floor. There was an old cornflake next to the bed. Angus pushed it with his toe, but it had grown roots, wiggling its way down into the carpet.

Bede half sat up. "What is it? What's wrong?"

"It's Mum," Angus said.

Bede flopped back against the pillow. His hand made scratchy noises as he rubbed his chin. "Leave her. She'll be fine."

Angus stared at the cornflake.

Bede groaned. "Fine." He kicked the blankets aside but they clawed at him. His feet pedalled, making the sheet go round-and-round-and-round. "Dammit!" Bede tore the covers off and swung his legs over the side of the bed.

"Okay." Bede ran his hands through his hair. He looked at Angus. "Come on."

Angus looked through the glass door to the dining room. The lights were off. Their mum was still at the table, her hands making-a-prayer in front of her.

Bede pulled at the hair on his stomach between his belly button and the waist band of his boxer shorts. The skin underneath made little pointy mountains as the hair pulled it up.

Bede made a noise in his throat and pushed Angus' arm. "Go back to bed."

"But—"

"Just go, Angus!"

A bit of Bede's spit landed on Angus' cheek. Angus rubbed at his eye trying to get it off.

Bede sighed. "Please don't cry, Gussy."

Angus dropped his hand from his face and stared at Bede. He wanted to tell Bede that there were no tears inside of him, but Bede's head wasn't tilted to the side like the teachers' were when they were Being Sympathetic. It was hanging down on his neck, staring at the ground.

"Go to bed, Gussy." Bede's voice went quiet. "It's all right. I'll…"

He waved his hand towards the dining room.

Angus nodded. He watched as Bede walked through the glass door and sat down next to their mum. Bede touched her shoulder, but she didn't look up.

***

Angus made himself a bowl of cereal for breakfast, but he didn't feel like eating.

Bede kept opening Mum's bedroom door and peering in. "It's okay, little man," he said. "Mum's just tired from sitting up all night.

She'll be all good to pick you up this afternoon."

Bede's voice was pretend-cheery, which made Angus nervous.

"Go on," Bede said. "Go get dressed, Gussy."

When Angus came back, Bede was on the phone. "Yes..." he was saying. "If you could just come and check on her..." Bede stopped as he noticed Angus. "Yes ... thank you, Mrs Appleton."

Bede was using his polite phone-voice. Mrs Appleton was Cassie's mum. Bede didn't like her normally.

"Don't you know it's rude to listen to other people's conversations, Gussy?" Bede said as he put the phone down.

Angus shook his head.

Bede nodded towards the door. "Come on, Gus. We'd better get to school."

Bede didn't say anything as they walked; he just listened to his head phones and made scowls with his face.

***

Angus waited in the classroom for his mum to pick him up. Bede had said she would be "all good to be him up this afternoon" and so he waited even though it didn't seem like she was coming.

Then there were no more kids in the classroom, and the halls were all quiet and empty, and Mum still wasn't there.

Angus followed the crack in the lino all the way to reception. He didn't tightrope-walk his feet though. He sat down on one of the chairs outside the principal's office.

Angus could hear the clock ticking above him. He knew Bede had sat here lots and lots of times before. Bede had talked about that clock ticking. In a minute, Bede had told him, the principal would come out to see him. He would tip his head to the side and sigh and he would run his hand across his shiny head. Then he would look at the clock and stare at it before pinching the bridge of his nose.

Bede said he did the same thing every time.

Bede was always disappointing Mr Dumpty, according to Mum. Bede told Angus that their mother was disappointed in him too. That's why she was the way she was. Because of him, not Angus.

Angus didn't believe Bede. He knew Mum was the way she was because of her, not because of them. Well, maybe a little because of Dad as well. But that wasn't Bede's fault either.

Miss Periwinkle from reception had bright, bright lipstick on, like she'd coloured her lips in with pink felt-tip pen. Angus thought maybe she was pretending not to notice him. She didn't like it when the Mums were late because then she had to look after the kids left behind.

Angus' mum wasn't normally late. She was always early or on-time or had Bede pick him up. Or at least, she used to be always early or on-time. Now she was just mostly on-time.

Mum had Bede pick Angus up more often than she used to too. Sometimes Bede had to say pretend-sorries because she thought she had told him to pick Angus up but she hadn't.

Angus shook his head. Mostly his mum wasn't late.

The chairs outside the office were shiny and sticky and they made Angus' legs hurt where they sucked at his skin. Except for the bit where the stuffing was coming out, which wasn't sticky, just tickly.

Miss Periwinkle looked up at Angus and smiled. "Where's your mum, Angus?"

Angus shook his head. "I don't know."

Miss Periwinkle nodded. "I'll give her a call, shall I?"

Her pink lips smiled at Angus as she dialled the phone, but her eyebrows joined together in a BIG FROWN. She made a noise in her throat. "No answer." She put the phone down and looked at Angus.

"Did Mum say Bede would pick you up today, Angus?"

Angus shook his head.

"Does Bede have a cell phone? What's the number?"

Angus gave Miss Periwinkle the number. He could hear her talking on the phone to Bede, but he didn't listen. Instead he wrote in his reading book: *It is rud to lizten to othr peples confersayshuns.*

Even though Angus wasn't listening he could hear that Miss Periwinkle was saying a lot of "Hmmms" and "Oh dears."

He wrote again in his book:

It is rud to listen to uther peoples conversayshuns.

It is rude to lizen to uthr peples confersaishuns

It is rood to liizten to other peples con...

Miss Periwinkle sat down next to Angus. She handed him a packet of biscuits. "How about I wait with you until Bede gets here?"

Angus looked at the packet. "Mum doesn't let us eat chocolate biscuits."

Miss Periwinkle smiled. "It'll be our little secret, eh?"

When Bede arrived, he wasn't by himself. Mrs Appleton and Cassie, from next door, were there too.

Bede sat down next to Angus and his leg went jiggle-jiggle-jiggle and the spiky cuff around his wrist went flash-flash-flash. He gave Angus a hug, which made Angus scared because Bede never gave him hugs.

Mrs Appleton kept saying:

It's okay, Angus.

It's going to be okay.

And so Angus wrote in his reading book. *It is OK, Angus. It is goinng to be OK.*

Then Mr Dumpty came out of his office.

Angus waited for Mr Dumpty to tip his head. For him to look at the clock and pat his shiny head and pinch his nose. Instead Mr Dumpty sat down next to him.

"Angus," he said.

Angus shook his head. Miss Periwinkle was making sad faces which would have been funny, except Bede was making sad faces too and that wasn't funny. It was just scary and Angus was scared.

"Angus," Mr Dumpty said again. "We need to talk about your mum." Mr Dumpty was tilting his head in the Being Sympathetic way.

And then all the adults were saying things and the clock above Angus' head was ticking so loudly.

"It's going to be all right, Angus."

TICK

"Mum's just not very well."

"Everything's going to be okay."

TICK.

"You're going to come stay with us for a while."

"It's going to be all right, little man."

TICK.

"No, not like your dad. Your dad was a different kind of sick."

"You'll like it at our place. You and Cassie can play all the time."

TICK

"Mum's not going to die. She just needs some time to rest."

TICK

"Gussy?"

TICK

"Come on, Gussy, talk to us."

TICK

Cassie hopped up onto the chair next to Angus. She stuck her thumb in her mouth. "When you come stay with us, can I hold Bruno?" she asked.

Angus didn't look at her.

Cassie took her thumb out of her mouth and wiped it on her dress. "I didn't tell Mummy I saw Bede smoking," she said. "You said I shouldn't."

"It's not because of us," Angus said and then he started to cry.

Splintered

He was crying over a splinter in his thumb. The day had been long, and the adults were secretly lamenting the lack of alcohol. Birthday parties for two-year-olds would be more enjoyable if there was alcohol, they imagined.

The offending shard of wood came from one of the toothpicks stabbed ruthlessly into the bodies of unsuspecting cheerios, and so at first it had been difficult to distinguish between the red of blood and the red of tomato sauce. He stopped crying when placed in a paddling pool and given a piece of birthday cake. They tweezed the splinter from his thumb without him noticing.

His mother and father began to argue – ostensibly over the assembly of the flat-packed playhouse given to him by a relative neither of them liked – but like most arguments, the real cause ran deeper. His father was unaware of this, and thought the argument really was about the playhouse. His mother found a bottle of gin.

Mondegreen

Dear Jenny,
I love you. I'm sorry.
Marco

***

Marco's CDs sat in three boxes on the floor of Jenny's bedroom. The first box was all mainstream bands. Mostly rock and pop.

Ed Sheeran
Adele
OK Go
Lourde
Green Day

***

Marco was the one who told Jenny, that if you listened to Black Sabbath backwards, you didn't get satanic messages – you got a recipe for cake in French. She spent three hours typing different versions of what she could hear into Google translate before she realised he'd made it up.

Marco had felt pretty bad about that, especially as Jenny had ruined her dad's record player by running it backwards over and over.

A couple of days after that, Marco had turned up at her house with a new needle for it.

She found out later that he'd stolen it from one of the record players at his brother's shop. Marco never told his brother about it and so neither did Jenny. She was pretty sure he knew though. Every time she went over there he'd give her dirty looks, right up until the day of the funeral. He didn't look at her at all that day.

***

Jenny's friend Peter kissed her the day after Marco's funeral. Partly because they were both grieving, but partly because it was inevitable. They had been circling each other like hunting dogs for weeks now.

Jenny kissed him back, only because she knew that had been what she wanted before Marco died. She felt Peter's hand against the back of her neck – his palm warm and rough. She remembered the time she had got drunk at her friend's party, and Marco had held her hair back for her as she threw up.

"People in drunk houses shouldn't throw beers," he'd said. She'd laughed, even though it didn't make sense. His hands had been soft against her skin.

Jenny wasn't sure what she wanted now. She just kept shaking her head, as if that would somehow change things.

***

The second box was the indie bands. The alternative ones. And the bands whose genre varied, depending on where the store manager chose to place them, or on the mood of itunes on any given day.

Walk off the Earth
London Grammar
Daughter
Twenty One Pilots
Of Monsters and Men

***

Marco and Jenny used to listen to CDs together. He'd text her, or she'd text him, and they'd both press play at the same time.

Jenny liked that they'd fall asleep listening to the same songs.

After he died, Jenny would still send the texts. *Opshop,* she'd say and then she'd press play. Sometimes she'd wait for him to text back. The CD would whirr into silence, but still her phone wouldn't beep.

Jenny played his favourite albums. The ones he had known she didn't really like, but she had listened to just for him. He had hardly ever suggested those ones, even though Jenny knew sometimes that was what he had wanted to hear. Just like Jenny had never suggested *Florence and the Machine*, even though she loved them. She hadn't listened to their album in months now.

Marco's mum gave Jenny all of his CDs. She said Jenny would be the one who would appreciate them the most. Marco's mum didn't know that neither Jenny nor Marco ever bought an album without making sure the other got a copy too.

***

"I bought you a present," Peter said, the first day Jenny came back to school after Marco died. He handed her an MP3 player. "I thought it would be easier."

Jenny turned the bright-pink, glorified flash drive over in her hand. She thought of trying to explain how she and Marco had grown up running in and out of Marco's brother's shop. That they had spent every moment they could playing the cassette tapes, and records, and CDs until his brother would drive them out. That the CDs had been a choice, not an inconvenience.

"Pink's my favourite colour," she said instead, and thanked Peter politely for the gift. Then she put the MP3 player in the back of her locker and closed the door on it.

***

Marco had left Jenny a letter. That was why he was out that night, in the dark, in the rain. He was riding home from her house, where he had left the letter in the mailbox.

For a while, Jenny thought maybe it was a suicide note – that he had ridden his bike into the path of the truck on purpose.

She didn't tell anyone about this idea. She pushed it to the back of her mind and let it fester there.

***

The third box contained mix CDs, ones Marco had made himself. Some were marked with Jenny's name, some with Marco's own.

None of them were marked with playlists.

Jenny opened the box once. She looked at the disks with her name on, and wondered why he had never given them to her.

Then she shut the box and never opened it again.

***

Dear Jenny,
I want you to know that I'm sorry. I want you to know that this isn't your fault. I want you to know...

***

Dear Jenny,
I don't know what I can say. You're my best friend. I've loved you since the moment I met you. That day, at school when you sat down and tipped my crayons out across the desk? I wish I could go back to that moment. I wish I'd picked them up

for you. Instead I think you cried when they all rolled off the table, and ... none of this is what I'm really trying to say.

I'm sorry, Jenny, I'm so...

***

Dear Jenny,

I've tried so many times to write this, and each time I screw the paper up before I finish. What is there I can say?

I sent you a text tonight and you didn't reply. You're probably just asleep. You probably didn't hear your phone, but I can't help thinking you don't want to talk to me.

About today – if you want to go out with Peter then that's fine. I want you to be happy. You need to know, though, that I love you. I've always loved you.

I wish I could say that face to face. I guess it doesn't matter now, anyway. I guess none of this matters.

I'm sorry, Jenny, I'm so sorry. I wish...

***

Jenny smoothed the letters out over her knees. They were on blue notebook paper, like the letter he had left in her mailbox. On the bottom of the pages, there was an imprint from something else written on the same pad.

It looked like lyrics, probably from a song they had both loved. She could only make out one fragment of a line though: **Let you go.**

Marco's brother sat next to Jenny, watching her read the letters. She had wanted to take them home and read them alone, sucking each of the words from the page until they became a part of her soul. Instead she read them there and then, sitting in silence with Marco's brother as they tried to pretend the only thing joining them wasn't gone.

"I found them in his rubbish bin," he said.

Jenny nodded. The pages were creased from having been balled up.

"I guess he never–"

"No," Jenny said. "He never told me."

"Well..." Marco's brother's voice trailed off into a sigh. His name was Steven. Steve. Jenny would never think of him as that, though. He would always be "Marco's brother".

There were many things she could have said to him. She could have apologised for the stolen record player needle. She could have thanked him for giving her the letters. She could have asked him if he had been the one to pack up Marco's CDs – the one to meticulously arrange them by genre, and if he knew what was on the mix-CDs.

Or she could have asked him, if he had the same idea festering in the back of his mind as she did in hers.

Instead they sat in silence.

Both of them thinking about Marco.

***

Marco's favourite song was *Everything you Want* by *Vertical Horizon*. Jenny didn't remember when he told her that. She hoped she didn't laugh at him, or scoff or anything like that. She couldn't imagine that she would have, but the fact that she couldn't remember made it feel like she must have blocked it out. Like perhaps she was so horrible to him, or made his face do that awful crumpling thing it used to do, that she'd forgotten – just to protect herself from feeling bad.

Jenny thought she must have listened to that song so many times before, without really hearing the lyrics. It was a song about a boy who loved a girl. A song about a girl who didn't love him back. Now when Jenny listens to it, she gets it.

She wished she could remember the moment he told her about that song. She wished she could remember the moment he had tried to tell her, and she hadn't heard him. Did he stare at her, waiting for her to understand? Did he press play and walk away, and just hope that she'd make sense of the lyrics herself?

Or maybe he just text it to her.

Maybe he just text her the same song so many times, she figured out it was his favourite without him having to say anything.

***

Jenny taped Marco's letters to the underside of her bed. She laid them one on top of the other, in the order she thought he had written them. The letter he had left in her mailbox was on top.

Dear Jenny,
I love you. I'm sorry.
Marco

Then she penned her own letter – what she would have said to him if he had told her. She taped her letter facing his, so the lines could read each other.

***

The day Marco died, he had yelled at Jenny. She'd been late to meet him because she had wanted to walk home with Peter. Jenny had meant to text him to say she was going to be late, but she'd forgotten. Instead she sat outside the classroom, where Peter was stuck in detention, while Marco sat at her place waiting for her to come home.

She and Peter walked together and, by the time they got to her place, she had forgotten she'd been supposed to meet Marco at all.

"Do you want to come in?" Jenny had smiled and fluttered her eyelashes in a way she was ashamed of now.

Peter had grinned and followed her inside.

Marco was sitting at the kitchen counter. He smiled when Jenny opened the door, but then his face crumpled as he saw Peter.

"Marco, I meant to–"

He shook his head and grabbed his jacket.

"I'm sorry, I–"

"Forget it. Just forget it."

"Marco!" She could see he was crying, and she didn't understand why. She reached out, but he pushed her away.

"Are you blind or are you just stupid?" He brushed his tears away, as if he was angry with himself for crying.

Jenny shook her head. "I don't–"

"You're not stupid. You're just selfish, aren't you Jenny?" Marco nodded to Peter. "Go on. Why don't you go off and sleep with him? Act like a slut like the rest of the girls at school."

Peter pushed Marco away then. Jenny's face burned, and she couldn't look at either of them. Instead she locked herself in the bathroom and cried. When she came out, both Marco and Peter were gone.

That night, Jenny heard her phone beep. She knew it would be Marco.

She didn't answer.

***

Jenny text Marco *Vertical Horizon* and then she pressed play.

From her drawer, she heard his cell phone beep, but she covered her ears against the sound.

She tried to pretend Marco was at his house, pressing play, falling asleep listening to the same song as her.

Symbolic Death

On the morning Tabitha died, she noticed an ancient symbol depicting a Death Curse scratched into the soap scum around her sink. She felt a cold trickle of fear run down her throat. Or at least she interpreted it as fear. In reality it was just minty-freshness from the toothpaste she'd forgotten to spit out when she saw the symbol.

Tabitha wondered whether the symbol was an omen of her own impending death. She thought of all the things she had not yet managed to complete, such as her study of ancient symbols, and the irony was not lost on her.

Then her flatmate banged on the door screaming for her to "get out of the bloody bathroom" so she laughed, shook her head, and said out loud "Superstitious nonsense," before wiping the sink and heading to work.

As she died an unexplained death while she was eating her lunch later that day, the symbol flashed through Tabitha's mind. She wondered whether, had she taken its warning more seriously, she would have been able to prevent her own death. But she dismissed that thought because somewhere deep down Tabitha believed in fate, even if she called that "superstitious nonsense" too.

One thought that didn't flash through her mind, was the question of how the symbol had ended up etched into the soap scum in the first place. Perhaps Tabitha had drawn it there herself, an unconscious doodle after staring at symbols day in, day out. Perhaps it was mere coincidence, a random mark left by the day to day movement of turning the taps on and off.

Or perhaps her flatmate had scratched it there, copied from one of the pages Tabitha was forever leaving lying around the house, when he washed his hands after making Tabitha's lunch.

Death's Daughter

It wasn't a job anyone would choose.

That is to say, I wouldn't have chosen it. There were some who did, but they'd last a couple of days at the most. Usually, they'd start to show signs of madness and we'd have to return them to their old lives before it took hold.

I didn't have an old life to go back to. My dad was a Reaper, therefore I was a Reaper. They swore me in on my sixteenth birthday; I collected my first soul the next day.

No one congratulates you after your first day on the job as a Reaper. They give you quiet nods, pats on the arm. Gestures of sympathy, not praise.

Six months on, there wasn't even that. No one felt sorry for you after your two-hundredth soul. They just expected you to get on with it – exactly like they did.

That night I was technically off duty, except, in a job like this; you're never really off duty. If you're the closest and you feel someone going, you don't have a choice. Well, you do, but the choice is to leave the person shrieking in agony until someone else can get there or to get out of bed and go help them yourself.

The accident was right outside my house, so of course I was the closest. The girl's pain woke me. She screamed, over and over. I couldn't tell whether it was in her head or for real. I hoped it was in her head. It was easier when they were unconscious.

Ryan was supposed to be stationed in our area that night, but I couldn't feel him anywhere near. That didn't surprise me. It was like him to blow off his responsibilities, and I certainly wasn't going to sit there and wait for him.

I pulled myself out of bed. My hair stuck to the back of my neck, in a damp matted knot. I pulled a pink elastic band from my wrist and wound my hair into a half-bun.

It was raining outside. I shivered and considered going back for a jacket. The girl's screams made up my mind for me, and I jogged out onto the street.

She was unconscious, lying in the road. She would have seemed asleep, but for the blood at her temple. A man – a boy really –

crouched over her. He held her face in his hands and wept.

"Wake up," he was saying. "Wake up, Karen."

"It will be all right," I said.

His head shot up, and his eyes met mine.

I stepped back. He could see me. His face twisted, despair distorting his features into a mess of tears and mucus. "Help…"

In training they taught us about people who could see Reapers. Usually they were the ones dying. In the final few seconds, they would recognise us. The first time that happened, I cried and wouldn't go out again for a week. This was different.

"Help her!"

I knelt down beside the girl. He didn't know who I was. Of course he didn't. In the real world, Death did not wear floral pajamas.

"It will be all right," I said again. I moved my hand, ready to collect her soul.

He jerked, as my arm brushed his. "You're..." He shrunk away from me, then his eyes flicked towards Karen. He pushed me back. "You leave her be!"

I was wrong. He did know who I was.

I stood and backed away. My training told me I should leave, wait for another Reaper to arrive and finish the job. I searched in my mind for Ryan, but I still couldn't feel him anywhere near. Karen's screams tore through my brain and I stumbled and fell.

My hand was bleeding, I could tell that, but it was getting harder to differentiate my pain from hers. I touched my temple and felt blood there too. Her blood flowing from my veins – the connection had gone too deep.

I forced my eyes open. He held her cradled in his lap. She was icy-pale, her lips blue. Mine must be too by now.

The rain washed the road, but I could still see the tire tracks leading away. Karen's memory of the headlights blinded me. The car hadn't even tried to stop.

"She's in pain," I said to him.

He shook his head and wouldn't look at me.

I pulled myself up. "You can help her."

"Stay back!" He tightened his grip on Karen, pulling her close against his body. If I took her soul now, it would kill him too.

"Okay, I'm..." I hesitated. There wasn't much I could promise here. He knew very well my intention, and there was no point lying. "I don't want to hurt either of you," I said instead. "I want to help her, and I know you want that too."

He stared at me, and his Adam's apple bobbed as he swallowed. His breath rattled in his throat.

"Do you have a cell phone?" I asked him.

He nodded. "Yeah, I..." He reached for his jeans pocket.

"Good." I did my best to force a reassuring smile. "Call an ambulance. Tell them what's happened." I wanted to tell him to ring his parents too, but I didn't think I could bear listening to him tell them.

He loosened his hold on Karen, then stopped and eyed me.

"I won't do anything, I promise. Just make the call."

He let go of her enough to break the connection between them. *Never make a promise you can't keep*, my dad always told me. I could take her now, while he was distracted. If I did that, he'd blame himself forever. And I'd have to run as soon as I'd done it.

He hung up the phone. "They're coming now."

I nodded. My stomach hurt – she must have internal bleeding. My legs were going numb too. I moved forward while I still could. "Are you hurt?" I asked him.

He shook his head, but I could see the graze on his arm. Karen let me see her memory of him diving sideways out of the path of the car.

"It wasn't your fault," I said. "She doesn't blame you."

"Shut up, you don't know anything about her."

"Yes, I do." I grabbed his arm and let him see everything she was thinking. Memories of him, her family. Her smiling and laughing and crying.

He pulled away from me. "How did you do that?"

I shrugged. "It's how it works." I coughed and tasted Karen's blood in my mouth. "See?" I showed him my arm – the graze was on my skin now, not his. "How can you see me?" I asked him. He didn't answer. Chances are he didn't know.

He stared at his arm. The wound bubbled and crusted over, then smoothed out, returning to healthy skin. "You can heal her?" His eyes flicked between me and Karen. "You can make her better?"

I shook my head. "It's too late. I can heal her pain, but…" I sighed. "It's too late."

I didn't tell him that if he didn't make up his mind soon, I would die with her. The next Reaper would arrive and have two souls to collect, not one. If it was Ryan, he'd have no problem taking the boy's soul too.

Sooner or later, Ryan would say. *What difference does a lifetime really make?*

I remembered the time my dog had had to be put down. Dad told me he would be the one to collect her soul. I argued with him until he told me that the connection meant if he didn't, he would die too. I told him I didn't care and then I cried, not for my dog but because I had just told my own father I didn't care if he died.

Afterwards he asked me if I wanted to get another dog, and I told him no.

I didn't want to love something that was just going to die.

"You love her, don't you?"

He hesitated. I could see he did, but perhaps it had always been unspoken.

"She loves you." I let him feel the energy of it.

"She's my best friend."

"I know, I get it," I said, though I didn't. You didn't get much in the way of friends in the Reaper line of work. The closest I had was Ryan, and that was only because we were the same age. It was easier if you didn't care about anyone else.

"Tell me about her," I said.

I moved forward as he spoke. He told me about the day they met – their first day of school. He told me about the tricks they played on their mums and about the day they decided to become "blood brothers". How they argued over whether it should be called "blood brothers" or "blood siblings" until they both got infections where they'd pricked their fingers. He told me about what they were going to study at university and the flat they were going to get together. And he told me she was his best friend. That he loved her more than anyone.

"She's in a lot of pain," I told him. I let him feel it, but only for a moment.

"Yeah." He started to cry again, and I gripped his hand.

In the distance we heard the ambulance sirens. He met my eye, but I shook my head. "It's too late."

He nodded. I looked away as he leaned down to kiss her cheek. "I love you, Karen." He raised his head but didn't quite look at me. "Is it ... is it nice? Where she's going?"

I should have been honest and said I don't know. I should have told him we're more like couriers than anything else, and past a certain point, we have no idea what happens.

Instead I nodded. "It's beautiful."

He sighed. "Good."

I touched Karen's shoulder. The rain drops dribbled down her cheeks as if she were crying. She was still, except for her chest which rose and fell in shallow jerks. My hand hovered above her sternum. The sirens were so close now, the sound bounced off nearby houses and back to us.

The boy had his eyes squeezed shut, his breathing slow. I wondered if he would remember any of this later, or if it would all be like a dream to him.

Karen's body tensed, resisting me. I clenched my fist, giving me a firmer hold. "You're okay," I said to her. I think she tried to say something then, but it was too soft. Her thoughts were swirling now, disjointed words moving in bunches not lines.

She made a little sigh, and her body went still. I felt relief as the blood on my temple dried and the pain in my stomach eased. Her face relaxed, the muscles going slack as she let go.

Then I was filled with his grief.

I realised I was still holding his hand. I tried to pull away, but he gripped me tighter, pulling at me to ground himself.

I held him then, the way my dad had held me after I took my first soul, and I had cried until I felt I would die myself.

"It will be all right," I said again.

***

The ambulance officers couldn't see me, but they never could. They were around Death so much, I was just part of the atmosphere. Right now, I wished they knew I was there. As they worked on Karen, I could see the boy getting false hope. I wanted to tell them to stop. She was already gone.

The boy didn't look at me after they arrived. He kept his eyes focused on Karen's face. I wondered if he could still see me, or if now Karen was gone that was over.

I took a step back as they loaded her into the ambulance. Protocol said I had to stay with Karen until they pronounced her, but I knew no one would blame me if I left now.

The boy stepped back too. Normally the family would have to be peeled back from the dying person. I'd seen nurses no bigger than myself restraining people, to stop them from running into the operating room as if they could save their loved ones by their mere presence. He just stood, though, and watched as they prepared to take her away.

"She's gone, isn't she." His voice was flat. A statement not a question. He didn't look at me, but I knew he was asking me and not just the universe.

I nodded. "Yes. She's gone."

He was lit by the blue and red lights of the ambulance. They deepened the shadows of his face, alternating him between child and hollowed out old man as they flashed.

"Go with her," I said. It wouldn't change anything, but I knew enough about humans to know he would regret it if he didn't.

The boy sighed. He went to take a step forward, then stopped. "Can you tell her I love her?"

I wouldn't see Karen again. I had no way to pass a message to her, but in this case it didn't matter. "She already knows."

The boy closed his eyes and swallowed. He reached out as if to take my hand, but then pulled away without touching me. I watched as he climbed into the ambulance. He turned back, meeting my eye. It seemed like he was going to speak, then the ambulance doors closed, and he was gone.

Just like no one congratulates you on your first day, no one ever thanked you for your work as a Reaper. Not that most of them knew we were doing it, but they wouldn't have even if they could see us. I think this would be the closest I would ever get.

It was still raining, and I felt the drips mark cold pathways down the side of my face, washing away the dried blood.

"It will be alright," I said to myself.

The Temple of the Inner Light

Shirley and I peered out into the darkness at the man on our doorstep.

"Is this The Temple of the Inner Light?" he asked.

"No, this is my home!" Shirley said. She looked shaken, like the man had frightened her.

The cuffs and collar of his jacket were worn, leaving them frayed and white, and his shirt was crumpled. He was at the age where everything – skin, clothes, hair – appears grey.

His complexion was that of a graveyard, oozing sadness, drained of warmth.

"This is the address I was given?" He fingered the brim of a battered fedora, clutched over his chest. His nails were dirty, nicotine-stained.

"I'm sorry." I closed the door and watched through the window as he shuffled off down the street.

"I found those books in my room." Shirley's voice gave a squeaky crack.

"What?"

Shirley pulled the end of her plait. Her hair came loose, splaying out into a wild, thorn-bush halo. She chewed on her thumbnail. "Those books. Remember ...? The religious ones."

I shivered. *Religious ones* was putting it nicely. The books read like the manifesto of a cult. "Don't think about that now."

"How can I not? This flat, it's–"

"The flat is fine."

"It's not." Her throat rattled with a sob. "I know you feel it too. The nightmares–"

"Stop it, Shirley!"

***

As I lay in bed that night, I felt an overwhelming panic. The darkness weighed down on me, compressing my chest and leaving me gasping.

I got up and turned on the light. The room was still dim, the bare light bulb dusty no matter how many times I tried to clean it. I pulled back the curtains and stared out.

A man stood across the street, facing the house. He lit a cigarette and raised his face to the sky. I heard rain hit the roof. He lowered his gaze and for a moment he seemed to look straight at me.

I turned as I heard Shirley moving around in the other room. When I looked back, he'd gone. I peered down the street, but he'd vanished from view. I leaned against the window frame and closed my eyes.

"I think we should find another flat," I said to Shirley in the morning.

She stared at her cereal and didn't answer.

***

Shirley and I never did end up getting another flat together.

She went back to her parents and I moved in with some friends from university.

A couple of years later I passed one of those crazy evangelical groups preaching on the side of the road.

"There are those out there that don't want us to see the truth…"

I tried to rush past but one of the girls got in my way. "Excuse me…"

Her clothes were brightly-coloured and ragged. I shrank away as the wind slapped strips of fabric from her dress against my arms. She drew her hand across her face, pushing back her hair. It splayed out, wild and violent.

I looked up at her.

She raised her hand to her mouth and bit down on her thumbnail.

"Shirley?"

She stared at me.

I stared back. "What are you doing?"

She pushed a pamphlet into my hand. "Would you like to join the Temple of the Inner Light?"

Attack on the Heart

"I have trained my heart…"

She speaks of the organ as if it were a disobedient dog.

"It was after eleven o'clock…"

This is a monologue, not a conversation.

"I knew he was calling from a phone box. I could tell…"

What difference does it make?

"I have trained my heart…"

She's done this part already…

She is seated with her elbow resting lightly on the counter. She holds an invisible cigarette in her raised hand, and gestures with it to emphasise her points. The vowels are carefully enunciated, and her voice projects well beyond the head of the other shop assistant. I begin to wonder whether this is some kind of dinner theatre.

I slip off my gloves and wrap my hands around the cup in front of me. The taste of the tea makes my mouth pucker, but today I need the warmth.

I sneak looks at the woman, afraid to watch her openly.

She holds her head stiffly, her face turned away from me, yet I can tell she knows I'm listening.

Her posture seems an attempt at nonchalance. Instead she looks like someone who keeps very still, hoping no one will notice she's drunk.

"I have trained my heart…" she says again. Despite the theatrics there's real pain in her voice. I see her as she truly is: an older woman, jilted in love, hiding behind layers of make-up and hair-dye. Everything in this shop is just like her. Aging, discarded, unloved. Things that were once favourites, but have been pushed aside to make room for something new.

She adjusts her cardigan. I fidget with my own. Even indoors it's cold. I lean over my tea and breathe in, trying to warm my lungs. Instead I cough, the musk of second hand clothes catching in my throat.

I wrap my hands back around the tea. My ring clicks against the cup. I stare at it, then close my eyes.

Breathe.

Nothing else.

Just breathe.

I get up and lean against the rail surrounding the café area and look down at the rest of the second-hand store below. I resist a childish urge to spit on the heads of the customers below, then a more dangerous one to jump.

The store is too full of goods to encourage sales, but the owners appear to be either oblivious of the fact or are blatantly disregarding it. There's a lot of silver, all of it catching the light, reflecting miniature worlds against each other. Racks of old clothes line the walls, their colours dulled with age like everything else in the shop, assistants included.

I can see why they've been forced to start selling morning tea as a way to turn a profit. I wonder if mine will be the only sale they make all day.

The height of the mezzanine makes me dizzy and I have to step away from the edge. I sit back down, determined to finish my tea and scone. Not out of hunger, but out of duty to my mother. *You mustn't waste good food, Miriam!*

"I have trained my heart..."

The phrase has become this woman's battle cry, though what exactly she is fighting, I don't know. It's a strange phrase, as isn't the whole point that you can't train the heart? That it runs away, with or without you, dragging you along behind if it has to?

You have stolen my heart. David said that to me, early on when we first met. He said it softly, staring straight into my eyes, trying to pull new meaning from a worn out saying.

I didn't want his heart – not at first. It was as if I'd shop-lifted the body part, in an absent moment, and was now stuck holding it. I was painfully aware of my ability to break it, painfully aware that any attempt to give it back would shatter it. The broken heart cliché was apt. He had given me something fragile, and I was more than likely to be careless with it.

Of course her heart's broken... I overheard my mother telling a friend I was "in love" when I'd returned home after a meaningless fling. This was long before David, back when they were all meaningless flings. My heart was nowhere near broken. I wasn't in love, I just let her think that. Not a lie, I told myself, just a small departure from the truth. An affair was more acceptable if you were in love. *Her heart led her astray...* My mother wanted to fit me into the romance novels she read. She wanted to understand me. She didn't want to have to think of her own daughter as a slut.

Miriam! I won't have you using that word in my house...

I pop a sugar lump into my mouth, and let it dissolve on my tongue. My mother is fond of blaming things on her heart. Hers aches with both love and sorrow. She and David have that in common; heart aches.

I wonder, though, why the heart is given the responsibility of love?

Is it that in the end, everyone's heart fails? After the illness, the accident, the old age, it's your heart that decides whether you live or die. All your emotions stop when the echo of the last beat fades. Then, all the pain, anger and confusion are transferred to the ones left behind.

Maybe it's simpler than that. Maybe we just need something to blame.

I swallow the last of my tea. It's time to go. Time to stop delaying. I layer myself up. Scarf. Hat. Gloves. Jacket.

Somehow I still feel exposed. Somehow I feel ripped apart.

The jilted woman is still relaying her story. I pass the second shop assistant, standing as she has been the entire time, halfway out the door. She rolls an unlit cigarette between her fingers and forces a smile, as I reach the door. She appears disappointed I haven't bought a silver gravy boat, or some other useless item. She continues making the right noises yes ... mmm ... uh-huh as the story continues, and her eyelids fall in heavy blinks as she tries to feign interest.

I squint as the wind hits my eyes and nose, and liquid beads on my eyelashes. I pull my scarf up, trying to protect as much of my face as I can.

It's not like I imagined. When David and I decided to move here, I dreamt of English winters with white snow, squirrels and foxes. Instead I got greying slush seeping into my shoes, wind so cold it burnt, darkness at 4pm.

When I reach the hospital, I'm more numb than cold. My footfalls echo against the white walls, and I keep my steps even and steady in the corridors.

I sit down and wait in his room.

I feel uneasy alone with the man in the bed. He looks like David, but it's not him. If it was David, my heart really would break. It would have cracked in two the moment I saw him.

But I feel nothing.

So this man is not David.

The doctor arrives and makes a sympathetic face. I try to respond with a suitably desolate look. He wouldn't understand that this is not my husband.

The doctor sits beside me. I keep up the expected expression. It's hard when all I want to do is laugh at the absurdity of this.

"Mrs Jefferies, I'm afraid the tests were conclusive. David shows no signs of brain activity. Your husband is not going to recover."

I nod.

"I know this is very difficult, but David's driver's license indicates he wished to be an organ donor."

I nod again. The doctor pauses. He wants something from me.

"We need your permission."

I look away, close my eyes. "I shouldn't be ... not me." I stumble over the words.

"As his wife, you're his next of kin."

I shake my head. "Someone else..."

"He has no other living relatives."

Again a pause, a long one.

"I'll leave you alone to think about it."

I shouldn't be making this decision. His real wife should.

I stare at the wall, pressing my hand to my mouth. There's something stuck in my throat. I can't swallow. If this isn't David, where is he? Why did he disappear the moment this man turned up? I lean my forehead against his hand, trying to make myself feel something.

David's hands were always warm.

These are cold.

I don't feel anything. It's not him.

If everything that makes up a person ends when the heart stops beating, where is this man? His heart is still beating, but there's no one there.

"My heart goes out to her ... alone in a new country and her husband brain-dead ... I don't know how I'd cope."

I can hear the nurses out in the corridor. I want to scream at them "It's not David". I want to tell them to stop blaming their hearts.

I press my head harder against his hand. I feel his blood pulsing against my skin. Or maybe it's my blood pulsing under my skin.

I lift my head up from the bed as the doctor walks in.

"If it's what he wanted ... then yes, he should be an organ donor."

The doctor nods. He pats me on the shoulder and leaves me to say goodbye.

I sit for a while, watching the man with David's face. I wish he could tell me if I did the right thing. I'm listed as an organ donor too, but what does it really mean?

The machines make noise, but he doesn't. It reminds me of a dream I used to have, back when David and I were always talking past each other. I'd be swimming deep underwater, and I'd see him. His mouth would move, but I couldn't hear what he was saying.

We wasted so much time with his saying one thing and my hearing another. With him you always had to read between the lines. I was always the writing, while he was the blank white spaces.

I take the man's hand and squeeze it. Then I go and fill out forms with questions about body parts. I pause for a long time over "heart" then sign and let them take it.

I hear David's voice in my head. *You have stolen my heart.*

I walk away, feeling I've ended the man's life.

I walk home to the flat from which David is missing. I want to eat, but instead find myself standing in front of the fridge, staring and staring but seeing nothing.

I hear a car pull up outside. A delivery van probably. Flowers from home, for me to take into the hospital.

Instead it's a taxi. My mother gets out. I open the door and wait for the barrage of heart metaphors to start. Instead she just stands there. I don't look at her face. I don't want to see the sympathy I don't deserve.

"Do you want some tea? I've got Earl Grey, and I think I've got some biscuits..."

"Miriam..."

The shaking in her voice makes me look at her. She's pale, and her eyes are puffy. I stare at her, unable to look away.

"My baby ... come here." She holds me.

I feel stiff. Awkward. I keep thinking how strange it is to be called "baby".

"I promise you, he'll come through this."

I shake my head. "No ... no he won't."

Mum pulls back and looks at me. She holds my face in her hands.

"He's dead. David's..." I can't say it. I start to shake. The man in the bed is David. David's dead. David's gone.

I'm crying, and my mother's holding me. I'm crying.

"He stole my heart" I say, and I feel my heart next to his ... beating ... beating ... beating.

Reviews

Enjoyed this book? You can make a big difference.

Reviews are the most powerful tool when it comes to getting attention for my books.

As an indie author, it can be hard to get my books into the hands of readers, but honest reviews help me do just that.

If you've enjoyed this book, I would be very grateful if you could spend just a few minutes leaving a review (it can be as short as you like).

Thank you very much!

Also by Helen

BROKEN SILENCE

A stranger just put Kelsey's boyfriend in a coma. The worst part? She asked him to do it.

Seventeen-year-old Kelsey is dealing with a lot – an abusive boyfriend, a gravely ill mother, an absent father, and a confusing new love interest. After her boyfriend attacks her in public, a stranger on the end of the phone line offers to help.

Kelsey pays little attention to his words, but the caller is deadly serious. Suddenly the people Kelsey loves are in danger, and only Kelsey knows it. Will Kelsey discover the identity of the caller before it's too late?

UNDERWATER

Bailey has a lot of secrets, and a lot of scars, both of which she'd like to keep hidden. Unfortunately, Pine Hills Resort isn't the kind of place where anyone can keep anything hidden for long.

When Bailey arrives, she just wants to get through summer quietly, spending as much time in the water as she can.

Then she meets Adam.

Bailey's not looking to make friends, but Adam isn't easy to ignore. Neither is his ex-girlfriend, Clare.

As Bailey grows closer to Adam, she draws Clare's animosity. Will Bailey be able to keep her past a secret, or will Clare discover and reveal the sinister truth about how Bailey really got her scars?

WE ALL FALL

Myra fell from the trapeze, and then she fell in love. Which one will hurt her the most?

Something is not right at the circus. Since Myra's accident, there have been an unexplainable number of falls, and a strange, hot wind whispering through the tents.

Then, a new fortune teller arrives.

Myra meets Giselle, the beautiful, blind, child fortune teller, who often speaks of spirits in a way which may or may not be a joke. Myra finds herself drawn to her, despite the fact that she doesn't believe in psychics.

When someone she cares about becomes the next victim of the falls, Myra must face the unnatural cause behind them.

Will Myra be able to save the people she loves, or will she be the next one to drop?

Find out about these books and more at www.HelenVFletcher.com

Acknowledgements

Thank you to everyone who read and commented on this collection, or on any of the individual stories. Your suggestions helped make this a better collection, and helped me see where bits only made sense in my head. Thank you also for answering all my questions about title, cover and all the other bits and pieces. Your feedback and reassurance has been invaluable.

Thank you to my friends and family who have supported and encouraged me in my writing journey. It's been a personal growth journey as well, and it's meant so much to have people backing me along the way.

About the Author

Helen Vivienne Fletcher has worked in many jobs, doing everything from theatre stage management to phone counselling. She discovered her passion for writing for young people while working as a youth support worker, and now helps children find their own passion for storytelling through her creative writing business, Brain Bunny Workshops. Helen is the author of three picture books for children, one short story collection, and two young adult novels. She has won and been shortlisted for several writing competitions, including making the shortlist for the 2008 Joy Cowley Award, and in 2015 she was named outstanding new playwright at the Wellington Theatre Awards. Helen's poetry and short stories have appeared in various online and print publications, and she regularly performs her spoken word pieces around Wellington.

Overall, Helen just loves telling stories, and is always excited when people want to hear or read them. You can find Helen at www.helenvfletcher.com or connect with her on Facebook.